ONCE UPON A STAR

A STAR LAKE ROMANCE #2

LORANA HOOPES

Edited by
JENNA BRANDT

Thank you so much for picking up this book. I hope you enjoy the story and the characters as they are dear to my heart. If you do, please leave a review at your retailer. It really does make a difference. Below are my other books, I would love for you to check them out, and if you'd like to stay informed about books or contests I might be having, please come join my newsletter.

The Heartbeats series:
The Power of Prayer
Where It All Began
When Hearts Collide
A Father's Love

The Star Lake series:
When Love Returns
Once Upon a Star
Love Conquers All

Kindle World series:
Love Breaks Through

The Wishing Stone Series:
Dangerous Dinosaur
Dragon Dilemma
Mesmerizing Mermaids
Pyramid Puzzles (coming soon)

The Lawmakers series:
Lawfully Matched (releasing 2/8/18)

CHAPTER 1

*a*udrey stared at the nurses leaning over the silver table, obscuring the view of the thing she wanted to see most.

"Are you ready, Mom?" The head nurse turned to Audrey, a tiny blue package in her arms.

Mom. The word had never applied to her, and she wasn't sure it fit. Was she ready? Probably not. Would she ever be completely ready? Probably not. But that didn't change reality. She tucked a strand of blond hair behind her ear and nodded.

"Here's your son." The nurse held the swaddled bundle out to her. Audrey opened her hands, unsure of what the nurse wanted her to do. The nurse's face softened and her warm brown eyes sparkled. With one hand, she adjusted Audrey's arms to place the tiny bundle in them. "Hold him like this." She demonstrated the proper technique. "You always want to support his head."

Audrey nodded, trying to keep her arms from shaking. She was afraid to breathe, afraid to move, but mostly afraid she'd drop the infant, so she kept her eyes glued to him. Would he shatter like a piece of glass? The image sent a shiver down her spine. She didn't want to find out.

The nurse's eyes twinkled as she watched Audrey adjust and readjust her holding position. "There is a bassinet here." The nurse pointed at a clear plastic tub that looked like a large shoe box on top of a wheeled table. It didn't look comfortable to Audrey, and she wondered how a baby slept in it. "If you want to take him walking, you need to put him in the bassinet, okay?"

"Do I hold him the rest of the time?" As much as she was enjoying the baby in her arms, what happened when she needed to sleep or use the bathroom?

The woman chuckled. "You hold him as much as you want and put him down when you need a break. We'll come in every few hours to check on you, and we'll show you how to change his diaper and dress him. You'll be a pro before you know it. Don't worry." She patted Audrey's arm like her grandmother used to when she asked a silly question, and then the nurse walked out of the room, still smiling and shaking her head.

Audrey's eyes dropped to the sleeping baby. His shock of dark hair reminded her of his father, the olive-skinned Italian who had charmed her with his fast tongue. She hoped it was the only trait Cayden would get from him. The world didn't need another heartbreaker. "I have no idea what we'll do, Cayden, but we'll figure something out."

Blake turned the glass on the countertop and glanced up at Max who leaned against the back counter, arms folded across his chest as if he were waiting for the answer to a question. The green of his plaid shirt matched the faded ball cap turned backwards on his head. "Sorry, did you say something? I'm distracted; it's just getting close to Christmas, and I miss Connie." A vision of the day she left popped into his head.

Blake opened the door, expecting to see Connie on the other side in her Sunday best. The church service started in half an hour. Though Connie stood there, his smile faded as he took in her jeans and t-shirt. There was no requirement of the patrons to dress up, but Connie always wore a dress or skirt. "What's going on?" Blake asked.

Connie bit her lip and her eyes fell to the ground. "I wanted to say goodbye."

"Goodbye?"

"I can't stay any longer, Blake." Her eyes lifted to meet his, and he saw the shimmer of liquid in them. "I hoped I could make a life here, but I'm a city girl. I miss the lights and night life. I miss the excitement."

"But, we were discussing marriage last week." Blake struggled to make her words compute in his brain.

"I know," she nodded, "and that's what got me thinking. The thought of living the rest of my life here is depressing, so though I love you, I have to say goodbye." She leaned in and pecked his cheek before flashing a sad smile and walking back to her car.

With a heavy heart, Blake watched her drive away before shutting the door and leaning against it. His brain tried to make sense of her departure.

"I get it," Max said, leaning forward and dispersing Blake's memory. "It's not the same, but you're welcome to spend Christmas with Layla and me.

Blake offered a half smile. "I'll consider it, but it's

your first Christmas together. You've been in love with that woman since I've known you and I don't want to be a third wheel. Besides, I'll probably hit the Christmas Eve service at church and spend the day with my mom. She's been lonely without my father around."

Max shrugged and turned back to the kitchen to finish serving the lunch crowd.

Blake took a bite of his hamburger, but while he knew it was delicious—Max was known for his burgers—it held no taste in his current mood. He fished a few dollars out of his wallet, laid the money on the counter, picked up his coat, and walked out the door.

The McAllister development where he worked sat a mile up the road, but as he still had fifteen minutes remaining on his lunch break, he decided to walk through downtown. His own house resided on the quiet outskirts of town, so other than hanging out with Max at The Diner, he didn't spend much time in the downtown area.

Blake pulled his coat tighter as the winter air bit through the heavy wool. Star Lake generally received one or two good snowfalls every winter, and though Christmas was still a few weeks away, the chill in the air made him believe the first snow was coming.

He didn't mind the snow, but he enjoyed it more when he had someone to share the experience with. Curling in front of the fireplace alone held little appeal.

Audrey shoved the last item in her suitcase and pushed down on the bulging bag as she tugged on the zipper.

"Where are you going to go?" Desiree asked, leaning against the doorframe.

Desiree was Audrey's roommate, and the two were about as different as night and day. Where Audrey was pale and blond, Desiree had darker skin and long dark hair.

"The only place I can," Audrey said with a sighing. "Home."

The thought held little appeal. Her wealthy parents had given her access to her trust fund at eighteen, and Audrey had opted to move to LA to try her hand at acting. At first, it had been fun. She'd found a few jobs and been in a few commercials, but then the jobs had become fewer and farther between, and after she ended up pregnant, they had dried up completely. Now all the money she had saved was almost gone.

Desiree's nose scrunched in disgust. "You'd go back to that tiny town, why?"

"I haven't had a job in months Dez, my savings have run out, and I can't go to work without someone to watch Cayden. If I go home, I can get help from my parents until I get back on my feet."

At least she hoped they would help. They hadn't been too happy when she decided not to go to college, but she didn't think they would turn their grandson away, even if they didn't want to help her.

Desiree shrugged and flicked her hair behind her bony shoulder. "Nothing in the world would make me return to my crappy hometown."

Audrey knew Desiree's home life had been rough, but while she hadn't wanted to grow up under her mother's thumb, it hadn't been a bad childhood. "I don't know if I'll ever be back, but I wish you luck."

After a quick hug, Audrey picked up Cayden's car seat, slung her bag over her shoulder, and left the apartment she had called home for the last few years.

CHAPTER 2

Audrey stood outside the mansion, her heart a lead anchor in her chest. She ran the possible options one more time, desperate for a new solution, but nothing came to mind. Her last five hundred dollars had paid for the flight and the rental car, so even if another way had existed before, it was gone now.

Her finger trembled as she pressed the ornate gold doorbell.

A young woman in a pale pink uniform answered the door. Though her face was unfamiliar, her position was not. Audrey's mother had always insisted on help.

"Can I help you?" The woman's even and friendly tone didn't mask the sadness in her eyes. Audrey knew that expression too well. Though she loved her mother, Evelyn's overbearing personality and her obsession with money and status often left those around her feeling drained and empty.

"I'm Audrey. Is Evelyn home?"

The woman's eyes widened at Audrey's name. Her mother must have informed even the newest help of her wayward daughter, but the woman said nothing, just nodded politely and motioned Audrey to follow her.

Audrey stared at the threshold. If she stepped over the line, there would be no turning back, and the anchor on her heart pulled ever tighter. Was this the only way? Audrey hadn't even spoken with her mother yet, and still she felt the imaginary noose tighten around her neck. Her throat dried up, and she closed her eyes to calm the beating of her erratic heart.

"Are you all right?"

Audrey's eyes flicked open. The young woman stared at her as if she were crazy, which perhaps she was. This was her mother for goodness sake, not an ax murderer. After another deep breath, Audrey forced her foot into the grand foyer.

It was exactly as she remembered it. The wooden floor gleamed a bright amber color, and the white marble columns sparkled as if they had just been cleaned—which, considering Evelyn's hatred of dust and clutter, they probably had been. A glass chandelier sent reflections of rainbows across the room though they didn't lighten the oppressive mood that filled the room. Over the marble fireplace, a portrait of the family done ten years ago stared back at her.

The sullen girl in the portrait sent shivers down her spine. She had looked so petulant. Getting away from her parents had been good for her. The freedom of the past years had erased the scowl from her face and straightened her shoulders. If only she could have stayed away.

"Wait here." The woman pointed to the white leather couch Audrey had once considered spilling grape juice on just to spite her mother. "I'll go get Mrs. McAllister."

The family in the picture continued to rain judgement on Audrey as she perched on the edge of the couch feeling like a schoolgirl waiting to see the principal. She glanced at the car seat on the floor beside her, thankful Cayden had fallen asleep before she pulled up to the house. Evelyn wouldn't tolerate his noise well.

The clickity-clack of heels on the hardwood floor sent an icy tremor through her body. Audrey drug her eyes from the sleeping infant to the hallway entrance. Her mother, with her brown hair perfectly in place and a string of pearls accenting her immaculate beige suit, stepped into the room.

"To what do I owe this pleasure?" she asked. The words sounded polite, but the cool inflection behind them told the real story.

Audrey stood, blocking the car seat with her legs. Evelyn hadn't appeared to have noticed it yet. "Please sit, Mother, I need to ask you a question."

Evelyn's lips pursed, and her eyebrow arched on her forehead, but she smoothed her skirt and sat in the straight-backed chair across from the couch. "What is it? It must be important. We haven't seen you here in what three years?"

Four. Audrey had come back for Elliana's wedding four years ago, but there was no need to point that out. Ignoring the dig, Audrey cleared her throat and proceeded with her rehearsed script. "I know you didn't approve of my going to Hollywood to pursue acting, but I needed to follow my dream."

"It must have gone well if you're back here." The sarcasm dripped from her mother's voice.

"Please let me finish. LA was amazing, but I made a mistake when I fell for a man who I thought loved me. I ended up pregnant, but he left me." Audrey stepped to the side, clearing the view of Cayden's car seat. "I kept Cayden, but I couldn't continue working."

Evelyn blinked but remained silent, waiting for the question.

Audrey gritted her teeth and took a deep breath. "I'm wondering if I can borrow money to hire childcare until I get back on my feet."

"Let me get this straight," Evelyn began once Audrey finished. "You've been gone for nearly ten years, and now you're only here because you need money?"

Audrey swallowed the irritation threatening to bubble over and answered through clenched teeth. "I wouldn't be here at all if it weren't for Cayden, but I've had no jobs the last few months and therefore no money to pay for help, so yes I am asking for money."

"No," Evelyn said, folding her hands on her lap.

"No?" Audrey narrowed her eyes, sure she heard her mother wrong.

"That's right, no. You were given money, which you squandered when you ran away to Hollywood."

"I was there for ten years."

Evelyn held up her hand, cutting off Audrey's protest. "If I give you the money, you learn nothing, but I can't have that baby going hungry either, so here's what I'm offering. I will give you enough to get a place as I'm assuming you would not accept my offer to live here, but then you will work for your father."

Audrey's head shook before Evelyn had finished. "Mother, no. I can find a job." Her father owned a development company, and Audrey knew nothing about it. Her passion had always been the stage.

"It's my money, so I get to set the conditions. Take it or leave it." Evelyn stared evenly at Audrey.

There were no options. Audrey needed the money and maybe working for her father wouldn't be too bad for a short time. Once she saved up enough money, she could always find something else. "Fine, Mother, is there anything else?" She didn't want to ask, but she feared a secret condition could come back to bite her.

"You have dinner here once a month."

Audrey bit the inside of her lip and closed her eyes. Once a month. She could handle once a month. "Fine, Mother," she said, opening her eyes. "You win."

"Very well. Julie?" The blond woman reappeared in the entryway.

"Yes ma'am?"

"Get me my purse."

Julie nodded and hurried away.

"I expect to see you at dinner next Friday," her mother said as Julie returned with her purse. Evelyn pulled out her pocketbook, and after rifling through it for cash, which she handed to Audrey, she filled out a check, tearing it from the register with an exaggerated slowness. "I assume you don't have a bank account here yet, so the cash is to help get that started. The check should cover your first month's rent, deposit, and household necessities."

Audrey mumbled a quiet thank you as she took the money. It felt like dirty, blood money in her hand, but she had no other choice.

"We'll give you the rest of the week to get settled, but your father will expect you at work at eight a.m. Monday morning."

"Yes, Mother."

Evelyn had never been a hugger, but she tilted her left cheek up in expectance of her obligatory kiss. Audrey planted a quick one, her lips stinging as if she had just made a deal with the devil.

The money burned in her pocket as she gathered up Cayden's car seat and headed back to her car.

CHAPTER 3

"*D*id you hear the news?"

Paula leaned over Layla's table three spots away, but her loud voice carried across the interior of the small eatery. The Diner was known for two things: Max's amazing food and being the hub of gossip, though Max hated that everyone congregated in his establishment to share news.

"No, but everyone will now, Paula," Max said with a raised voice from the front where he was wiping the bar counter after the lunch rush.

Paula shot him a dirty look before turning back to Layla. "Audrey McCallister is back in town."

Blake's pulse stopped at the mention of Audrey's name. He placed his coffee on the table top and leaned forward to eavesdrop on the conversation.

"And she has a baby," Paula continued.

As quickly as it flourished, the happiness in his heart fizzled as if doused with water. If Audrey had a baby, then a husband probably existed as well.

"That's nice," Layla responded. "I'm glad she's happy."

Paula's eyebrow arched up her face, and she jammed her hands on her thick waist as she shook her head. "I didn't say she was happy. The rumor is her man dumped her, and she came home for financial assistance."

Blake's heart lifted with the news Audrey was free, but a twinge of sadness remained for the hardships she must have faced.

"Well, the past is the past," the ever-enigmatic Layla said as she smiled up at Paula. She often avoided conflict and chose the higher road. "I say we welcome her with open arms and remind her what a great town Star Lake is."

Paula had the decency to look abashed as she squared her shoulders. Her nose tilted in the air and her dark hair swirled with the flick of her head. "Of course we will. I'm sure we'll see her around as the word is she rented a place in town and will be working for her father."

Blake's eyes dropped to his coffee to conceal his excitement. Audrey McCallister was not only back in town, but she would be working at her father's office, the same office he entered every day. Though he had been too shy to tell her his feelings in high school, perhaps now he would find the courage.

A udrey set Cayden's car seat on the living room carpet and glanced around the small house. The odor of paint still hung in the air, along with the scent of carpet cleaner. Though not huge, the two-bedroom house was in good shape though bland with tan wall to wall carpet and white walls. The kitchen continued the theme with white laminate flooring and brown cabinets.

"Well, Cayden, it isn't much, but this is home for now," she whispered down to the sleeping infant.

Tomorrow, she would have to get furniture–a crib for sure, a bed for her, some chairs and a table, but tonight they would sleep on the blankets she had brought from her old apartment. Blankets, clothes, and baby necessities were about all she had been able to bring on the plane.

She added furniture and groceries to her mental to-do list, along with a cheap car. Audrey had sold hers to help pay for plane tickets. The sheer enormity of the growing list elicited a sigh from her as Cayden continued to sleep. Jealous of his lack of responsibility, she tiptoed out of the house to grab the blankets and clothes from the car.

When the bags were all inside, exhaustion settled on her shoulders and Audrey yawned. She wanted to curl into a ball and sleep for a week, but she knew it wasn't a possibility. Her internal sensor told her Cayden would be up soon to eat, and after that, she was sure sleep would be slow in coming as sleeping on the floor had never worked well for her.

The morning light peeked in the open windows early the next morning. Curtains or blinds. She would need those too. Audrey tried to squint her eyes shut, but it was no use. Her stomach growled in frustration; she'd have to get up soon to feed it. At least she had thought to make a quick stop at the market downtown yesterday, and coffee and cereal waited for her in the kitchen.

Stretching her arms, she tried to work the kinks out of her neck. The hard floor had taken a toll on her body, and every joint crackled in agony.

Cayden laid spread eagle beside her. He had

woken like clockwork every two hours to eat, but thankfully he'd fallen back asleep quickly each time.

With as little noise as possible, Audrey struggled to her feet. A shooting pain spiraled down her back as she tried to stand upright, and she leaned back to stretch the knot out. When her shoulders returned to their normal position, she tiptoed into the kitchen to make her breakfast before Cayden awoke.

The bright white of the kitchen hurt her tired eyes, and she squinted them shut as she rummaged through the bag from the market. She hadn't picked up much, but small plastic bowls, a mug, and spoons had been at the top of her list. Cereal and coffee were staples in her life.

She ran the bowl under hot water to clean it, wishing she had remembered soap yesterday at the store. Another item she would have to add to the list for today's trip. Along with paper towels, she realized as she turned off the water and waved the bowl in the air to dry it off.

Coffee. That was what she needed. A nice, steaming mug of the hot liquid would kick her brain back into gear, but as she turned around, she realized she hadn't picked up a coffee maker either. With a sigh, she grabbed the cereal from the bag and filled the bowl before adding the milk from the very bare fridge. She'd have to make a caffeine stop, or she wouldn't make it the rest of the day.

Cayden woke as Audrey placed the rinsed-out bowl in the sink. After feeding him, she ran a quick brush through her long blond hair before piling it onto her head in a loose ponytail. She needed a shower in the worst way, but she had to tackle this list first.

After changing out of last night's clothes into a sweater and a pair of jeans—the temperature was much cooler here than in California—she loaded Cayden up in the car.

Her first stop was the Goodwill on the outskirts of town. Most of the groceries she could get at the general store in Star Lake, but they wouldn't have the furniture she needed. Luck was with her as she found a sturdy crib, a comfortable couch and bedframe, a decent dining room table, and a few scratched tables. The store even agreed to deliver the items later that afternoon for a nominal fee and gave her the name of someone they knew selling a gently used mattress.

After buckling Cayden in again, she pointed the car back to Star Lake's downtown. The Diner was sure to have coffee. Whether it would taste good was another matter, but she doubted Star Lake had built a Starbucks or any other coffee joint for that matter. In fact, she doubted much had changed about the downtown at all. Star Lake seemed to live in its own bubble, away from time and passing trends.

Few cars lined the street as she pulled into a spot in front of The Diner. As she grabbed Cayden's car seat from the back, she noticed a new shop across the way. Sweet Treats Bakery. *Hmm, maybe a few things have changed. If The Diner's coffee is terrible, perhaps this new place will have a decent cup.*

The bell chimed overhead as she pushed open the front door. A man with slicked brown hair and a checkered shirt sat reading a newspaper at the back booth while Max filled ketchup bottles at the front. Though five or six years older than she, Audrey had harbored a secret crush on the broody owner through high school.

Max glanced up as she approached the counter. "Well, I'll be. Audrey McCallister. The rumor mill said you were back in town." A growth of stubble gave him a rugged look, and Audrey's heart fluttered in her chest.

She placed Cayden's car seat on the tile floor beside her before climbing into the barstool. "Hey, Max. It's good to see you. Let me guess, Paula?" She had taken a few dance classes with Paula in high school, and she remembered the busty woman often sharing tidbits of gossip.

"Who else?" he asked with a crooked half-grin. Audrey had never seen Max's actual smile. "Can I get you something? The breakfast rush just ended, but I could whip something up for you."

Audrey waved her hand, not wanting him to make a fuss for her. "I had cereal, but I could go for a cup of coffee."

With a swift nod, Max grabbed a mug from under the counter and poured in the murky black liquid. "I don't have any fancy creamer, if you wanted that. Presley, across the street, does more of the frou-frou coffee." He placed a cup of milk and a canister of sugar on the counter.

"Is she the owner of the bakery?" Audrey asked, looking over her shoulder in the direction.

"Yep, she moved back a few months ago. Evidently, she studied in Paris for a time, but it didn't work out. She makes good pastries too."

"Moved back? So, she lived here before?" Curiosity at meeting anyone else who had left town and come back burgeoned inside her. Perhaps it would help her feel less like a failure.

"Yeah, Layla said she was a few years behind us in school, so she'd have been a few years ahead of you I guess. I don't really remember her." Max shrugged and returned to filling the ketchup bottles.

"You still keep in touch with Layla?" Audrey tried to keep her voice even. She had known, even back in high school, that one reason Max was still single was that he adored the pretty Layla Matthews.

"Actually, Layla and I are together now." His hazel eyes pierced hers, and one side of his lip pulled up in a crooked smile—probably the closest thing he could do to a real one.

There was no mistaking the pride in his voice, and Audrey swallowed her disappointment. "That's wonderful, Max. I'm thrilled for you." As she turned her attention to the coffee to hide her reaction, he finished filling the bottles and took them out to the tables.

When her coffee was empty, and she felt a little more awake, Audrey plunked down a five-dollar bill, grabbed Cayden's car seat, and walked back to her car. He woke just as she snapped him in, so she climbed in the back seat next to him, pulled a bottle from her bag, and fed him. She had never gotten him to nurse and had been forced to settle on bottles.

After Cayden finished, Audrey climbed into the front seat. Though it would be a quick walk to the market, the heavy carrier made driving more appealing.

The general store parking lot was also mostly empty as most people were at work. Audrey was glad. If Max and Layla had stayed in town, then peers she went to school with might have as well, and she wasn't ready to face them yet.

After grabbing a cart and placing Cayden's carrier in it, Audrey entered the store. A young freckled-face checker greeted her as she passed, and she flashed a small wave before continuing to the produce section.

She piled bags of apples, oranges, lettuce, and peppers in her cart. She might no longer be in health-conscious Los Angeles, but she still wanted to regain her pre-baby figure. The extra twenty pounds she carried around now was a source of embarrassment and a hindrance on her outfits. Not to mention it was a constant reminder of why Tony —Cayden's father—had left her. As Audrey reached for a bunch of bananas, she heard a male voice speak her name.

Turning, she spied a sandy haired man with chiseled features and warm brown eyes. Though he looked vaguely familiar, she could not place how she knew him.

"Audrey McCallister, is that you?" His deep, rich voice flowed over her ears like silk.

"Yes, it's me." She paused, racking her brain one more time for a name. "I'm sorry, I feel I should know you, but—" she shrugged, letting the sentence trail off without an ending.

The corner of his lip twitched, forming a playful smile and highlighting a dimple in his left cheek. "Blake Dalton. We went to school together though I doubt you would remember me."

She wrinkled her forehead, running through the boys she knew in school. The name didn't belong to anyone who had run in her immediate circle, but an image of the skinny class president in glasses flashed in her mind. Her eyes widened as she made the connection. He looked so different, so. . . handsome.

Blake laughed at her reaction. "Yeah, I get that a lot. I worked out in college and put on some muscle. My job helps too."

"Oh, what do you do?" Audrey asked, visions of him modeling parading through her mind.

He blinked at her and tilted his head. "You don't know? I work for your father; I'm on his construction crew."

"Oh, I haven't spoken to my father yet. I just got into town two days ago."

A twinkle lit Blake's eyes as he nodded. "Yes, I heard that. . ."

"From Paula," they finished together and exchanged smiles before the awkward silence descended.

"Well, I'll let you get back to your shopping. I have to get back, but I'd love to catch up sometime." He nodded at her.

"I'd love that too."

As she watched him walk away, she couldn't help but admire how the years had treated him.

CHAPTER 4

"Good morning, sunshine," Audrey said, picking Cayden up out of his crib. She rubbed the sleep from her eyes with one hand, holding Cayden on her left hip. His wails lessened as he wriggled in her arms. Though she had assembled the crib, he had not enjoyed sleeping in it and had been up longer than normal between feedings.

"Let's get you fed, huh? It's only been"–she blinked at her watch, trying to make her tired eyes focus on the blurry image - "two hours. All right, you must be hungry."

She shuffled to the kitchen, flicking on the hall light as she went, and opened the fridge, grabbing a pre-made bottle. After shaking it up to mix the contents again, she popped it in the bottle warmer.

"It'll be ready in a minute," she said to Cayden. When the warmer dinged, she stuck the bottle in his mouth. Then she grabbed a k-cup pod from the cabinet she had stocked after her grocery run. With a quick flick, she loaded it in the new coffeemaker and punched the button, watching Cayden drain the bottle as the melodious dripping of coffee began.

The drip slowed like the end to a beautiful symphony before stopping. Yawning, she grabbed the mug and stumbled into the living room to the couch. After placing the mug on the end table, she plopped down on the couch with Cayden on her lap. As she reached for the aromatic liquid, a knock at the door sounded, and Audrey sighed and stared longingly at her drink.

"Now who could that be?" she asked Cayden as she stood and crossed the carpeted floor. Though his blue eyes considered hers, he continued to suck on his bottle oblivious to her question. She shifted him in her arms and opened the door.

A petite blond with her hair pulled back in a severe bun stood on the other side. Her grey suit rivaled many of Audrey's mother's. "Hello, I'm here for the nanny position." She held out a white sheet of paper, presumably her resume, with one hand. The other held a small black satchel.

"Excuse me?" Audrey blinked at her.

"The nanny position. My company said an order existed for nanny candidates to come to this address today at eight, so here I am."

Audrey sighed. It had to be her mother. Even when she wasn't helping, she was meddling. Audrey doubtless couldn't afford a true nanny, but interviewing them would at least allow her to see what was out there. "My mother didn't tell me what time she set these up," she said, playing along. Her face flamed as she glanced at her checkered flannel pajama pants and t-shirt. "I'm sorry. I haven't even dressed."

"That is fine," the woman said in perfectly proper English. "I assumed I would take care of the child in the morning while you got ready for work. May I come in?"

"Of course, I'm so sorry. Please come inside." Audrey stepped back, allowing the polished woman to enter.

Her heels sank into the carpet as she crossed the living room, and though she said nothing, her nose wrinkled slightly in displeasure.

The modest room was neat, but it was no fifth avenue penthouse. The furniture from the Goodwill was clean, but mismatched. No television sat featured in the room as Audrey hadn't found one at the Goodwill, and no art adorned the stark white walls. Audrey surveyed the room from the lens of the woman and swallowed her embarrassment. She must look atrocious and poor to this woman, who worked for wealthy families.

The woman eyed each furniture piece, deciding on the beige recliner. She perched on the edge of it as if afraid of catching something if she sat all the way back and set the satchel on her lap.

Audrey stifled a grin at her obvious discomfort. If this woman avoided a used chair, how on earth would she deal with a baby who spat up multiple times a day?

With perfectly manicured fingers, the woman opened the satchel and pulled out another white sheet and passed them both to Audrey, who took them before returning to the couch.

"My name is Tess Fairchild. As you can see, I have impeccable references. I believe in a strict schedule as I find it helps the child adjust easier. I arrive at seven to allow you to get ready for work, and I need to leave precisely at six. Though I clean up after children, I do not do other housework." She folded her hands in her lap. "Now, do you have questions for me?"

So many questions spawned in Audrey's head. Where did she even begin? "I should have questions, shouldn't I?"

Tess's head tilted to the right, and her right eyebrow arched, but she said nothing, just stared with an unwavering gaze.

"Okay, um, would you play with Cayden?" The image of this poised and proper woman crawling on the floor with a baby was laughable.

"I will make sure he has adequate play time."

That hadn't been her question, but it was probably the best this woman would give. "I guess that's it then." Audrey stood, signaling the end of the interview.

"Very well. I look forward to hearing from you." Tess smoothed her skirt as she rose from the chair and crossed the floor, stepping with her toes to keep her heels out of the carpet.

As Audrey closed the door behind her, Cayden finished the bottle. "Hungry, were we?" After setting Cayden on the floor for his tummy time, Audrey rinsed the bottle in the kitchen sink and placed it in the drainer.

On the way back, she spied her mug still steaming on the end table. With a relieved sigh, she picked it up and managed one glorious sip before another knock sounded at the door. Audrey rolled her eyes, placed the mug back on the table, and opened the door again.

A thick, elderly woman returned her gaze from the other side.

"Hello, I am Helga, and I am nanny." Her German accent made the words hard to understand.

"Of course you are," Audrey said under her breath, but Helga hadn't heard her as she had muscled her way past Audrey and into the living room.

"It is small. This is it?" she asked.

Audrey assumed she meant the house and nodded. "Cayden's room is down the hall. This is the living room, dining room, and kitchen space."

"Good, easier to keep clean. I do only light housework. Here are my resume and references."

Two more white pieces of paper appeared under Audrey's nose. Similar to the previous woman, the references on the resume were impeccable, but impersonal. Helga rattled off her rules, never bothering to sit down. Instead she paced like a predator stalking a prey. Her heavy footsteps sent shudders along Audrey's spine. She could not imagine Cayden spending all day with this large, fear-invoking woman.

He must have had the same idea because as Helga leaned over him, he let out a loud wail and flailed his tiny fists. Audrey picked him up, and as soon as she could, she ended the interview.

"Okay little one, let's change your diaper and lay you down for a nap."

After grabbing a diaper and some wipes from the nearby stash, Audrey laid Cayden on the carpet and unzipped his sleeper. Before she had gotten his legs out, another knock sounded.

"You've got to be kidding me," she whispered to Cayden. "Come on in, the door's unlocked."

"That's a good way to get robbed," Elliana, her older sister, said, poking her head in.

"Ellie!"

Elliana was three years older than Audrey, but the two had grown up close friends. After Elliana married and stopped coming around as often, Audrey was the only one for her mother to focus on. It was then Audrey became disillusioned with her parents' money and wanted a way out.

Audrey finished the changing and hugged her sister. "Sorry I didn't open the door for you; I figured it was another nanny."

"Yes, mother told me she lined candidates up for you."

The snort escaped Audrey's mouth before she could stop it. "Yeah, candidates I can't afford. She refused to lend me money to help pay for one."

Elliana crossed to the kitchen and placed her bag on the bar. With her dark hair, she was the antithesis to Audrey. Growing up, people had often asked if they were related. Audrey had taken after their mother's fair complexion, while Elliana had gotten their father's darker hair and skin. "Hand me my nephew."

"Ugh, I don't think I can handle more interviews," Audrey said as she handed the baby over. "Want to stay and help?"

Elliana pursed her lips, pretending to think before smiling and shaking her head. "Sure, why don't you go get dressed, and I'll get the next one." She pointed to the pajama pants and grinned. "I'm surprised they haven't gone running after getting a look at you."

"Ha Ha," Audrey said, but the smile remained on her lips. Though she hadn't missed her parents much, she had missed her sister.

As she reached her room, she heard Elliana open the door and greet the next nanny hopeful. The blissful silence in the room comforted Audrey, and she took her time changing clothes, relishing the momentary break from nannies and Cayden's crying.

From her drawer, she pulled out a pair of jeans, tugging them up over hips still puffy with baby weight. An oversized grey t-shirt went next to cover the jeans. Then she brushed her teeth and ran a brush through her hair before exiting the sanctuary.

"Thank you. We'll be in touch," Ellie's voice carried down the hall.

"But I was told to meet with Ms. Audrey McCallister," a woman protested. Audrey pressed herself against the wall so as not to draw attention.

"Well, Audrey was a little busy, but I assure you I will relay your information." There was a forcefulness in Ellie's voice that Audrey remembered from childhood. She had always envied that fortitude because Ellie had been better about standing up for herself, even against their mother. When the front door closed, she pushed herself off the wall and continued down the carpeted hallway.

"That was fast," she said as she rounded the corner.

"Eh, she wasn't the right one. Too stiff."

"They've all been too stiff so far. Mother put them together, remember?"

"And who could deign to deny Evelyn McCallister, right?" Ellie's chin tilted up in the air as she uttered the mocking statement.

"What am I going to do, Ellie? I can't afford any of these women." Audrey picked up the mug of coffee, hoping to swallow a little of the comforting nectar, but the cold liquid crawled back up her throat. With a shake of her head, she popped the mug in the microwave to warm it again. Before it finished the minute reheat, another knock echoed through the room. A frustrated sigh escaped Audrey's throat. Would she ever be able to finish this cup of coffee?

"Want me to send them all away?"

"I'd love that, but then what do I do?"

"Leave that to me." A playful smile curled Ellie's lips up at the corner and she crossed to the door. "Sorry, the nanny position is filled. You can all go home."

"What are you doing?" Audrey asked. "I told you I need someone to watch Cayden."

"Yes, but you have another option you haven't explored." Ellie's brown eyes twinkled with whatever secret she was toying with.

Audrey was too tired to play this game. "What other option, Ellie?"

The playful smile spread into a wide grin. "You have me." She held her hand up as Audrey's mouth opened. "Now, wait, hear me out. Phillip and I have no children yet. I live right outside town, and I want to get to know my nephew."

Though Audrey liked the idea, she worried about infringing on her sister. "I can't pay you much, at least not at first. I need to purchase a car, so I can return the rental, and it will be a bit before I get paid."

"That's fine. Phillip makes plenty of money, and I still have my trust fund. I don't need the money, and I want to help you out. I'm so tired of staying in the house, but a rich debutante with no skills isn't exactly in high demand these days."

Audrey opened her mouth to agree, but Ellie cut her off.

"Please, you know I'm good with kids. Let me try for a week, and if you hate me after that, you can call one of these cardboard cutouts." She flicked her hand at the stack of white papers.

"Of course I'll let you watch him," Audrey replied. "I can't think of anyone I'd rather have. I'm just worried about Mother finding out."

"You leave Mother to me if she finds out." Ellie flashed a conspiratorial wink, and Audrey smiled. Just like old times.

CHAPTER 5

*B*utterflies raced around Blake's stomach as he dressed for the day. The thought of seeing Audrey again had kept him awake all night, and he splashed water on his face to diminish the visible rings under his eyes.

The McAllisters had moved to Star Lake when Blake was a Sophomore, and his attraction to Audrey's beauty had been immediate. With her long blond hair and bright blue eyes, she was the epitome of cheerleader stereotypes, but even though she was wealthy and hung out with the richer kids, she was never mean to anyone, at least not that Blake witnessed. However, she'd also never tried to get to know those outside her social class, and so Blake had pined for her from afar.

Blake had known he'd had no chance with her

back then–the skinny, geeky kid with coke bottle glasses and checkered alligator shirts, but when he'd gone to college, he'd packed on some weight. When he'd found weightlifting, that weight had changed into muscles. His first girlfriend in college also set his fashion straight, throwing out his pocketed shirts and Levi jeans for the more popular variety and cutting his curls to make a manageable hair style. The dramatic effect had started a chain reaction. While the two of them hadn't lasted, he was forever grateful to her.

With a final glance in the mirror, Blake flicked off the light, grabbed his keys and lunch, and loaded up in his red Chevy truck.

Twenty minutes later, Blake pulled into the parking lot of McAllister development and parked in his usual spot. After locking the truck, he gathered his courage, pulled back his shoulders, and sauntered in the front entrance.

Audrey sat at the front desk, her lips pinched into a tight line. Her jaw clenched as the phone rang and she brought it to her ear. Though he could tell she was frustrated, she looked like an angel to him with her blond hair skimming her shoulders like spun gold. He wanted to say hello, to bring a smile to her face, but she was on the phone, and he had no real reason to stay in the lobby. His shoulders dropped as he drug his feet across the floor, hoping the caller on the phone would be quicker than his slow pace.

No such luck. The phone was still against her ear as he entered the door to the employee lounge where the check-in resided, but then inspiration hit, and a smile lit his face. A small coffee bar had been installed next to the cafeteria the previous month. Blake had never frequented it because he liked his coffee black and coffee from home was cheaper, but Audrey didn't appear a black coffee type of person. He didn't even know if she drank coffee, but he thought she would appreciate the gesture.

"Hey, good morning Blake," Wes, a fellow contractor, waved to him as he punched his card.

"Morning, Wes."

"Where are you hurrying off to?"

"I was going to try the new coffee bar. Is it any good?"

Wes's forehead wrinkled in confusion. "Yeah, but don't you bring coffee?"

"I figured I'd get a coffee for Audrey. She looks a little frazzled out there."

Wes' lips curled into an understanding smile, and he nodded, one eyebrow raised. "You hoping to impress the boss, huh?"

Impressing Audrey's father had never crossed his mind, but he preferred others thinking that rather than knowing his true reason of trying to win Audrey's favor. "It's not like that. I just want to welcome the new girl."

"Sure, whatever you say, man." Wes' laugh followed him out of the room as he made his way to the cafeteria. The lunch area was not a large room as many of the workers took their lunch elsewhere, but the open room housed several tables and a buffet line right near the kitchen. The coffee shop sat on the far end, closest to the outdoor entrance.

A mousy brunette glanced up at him from behind large glasses as he approached, reminding him of himself in high school. "What can I get you?" Her voice was so soft that he leaned in over the counter to hear her.

"What's the best drink for someone who may not like a strong coffee flavor?" he asked as his eyes scanned the menu. Mocha, frappe, latte–the words were all Greek to him.

"Um," the girl's face scrunched in confusion. "Well, I like my coffee sweeter, so I prefer either a mocha or a macchiato, but everyone's different."

"Which has fewer calories?" He wasn't sure if

Audrey was watching them or not, but if she was, he wanted to be prepared.

"A caramel macchiato is lower in calories."

"Great, I'll take that one please in a medium size."

"You mean a Grande?"

"Is that medium?" he asked, confused.

"Yeah," the woman nodded, a 'what rock have you been living under' expression on her face.

"Then, that one."

A few moments later, she placed a cup on the counter. "It's four dollars," she said.

Ah, yes, this was why he brought his coffee from home. How did people afford specialty coffee?

"Aren't you going to taste it?" she asked as he picked up the cup after forking over his money.

"It's not for me. It's for a friend." He flashed her a small smile and strolled back to the front entrance.

Audrey was off the phone, but her gaze was focused on the computer screen in front of her.

"I thought you could use a little pick me up," Blake said, tapping the top of her desk.

She glanced up at him, dark shadows circling her eyes. "Thank you. I told my father I did not know how to be a secretary, but he and my mother insisted I learn a skill. They don't consider acting a skill."

"Well, that's because they never watched you on stage." Blake flashed a smile, wishing he could bring one to her face. The memory of her playing Juliet their senior year still popped into his mind occasionally. He had never been a fan of Shakespeare but watching her on stage had made it tolerable.

A sad smile played across her lips. "Yeah maybe. Well thank you anyway. I gotta get back to this."

"Of course, I hope it gets better." He had hoped to ask her out, but now did not seem the right time. He would just keep praying for an opening to become clear.

CHAPTER 6

"*H*ow was the first day?" Ellie asked as Audrey dropped her purse on the floor and collapsed into the couch.

Audrey exhaled a giant sigh. "I don't think I'm cut out for secretarial work. Everything went wrong. The only positive part of the entire day was lunch and the coffee Blake brought me this morning."

Ellie's eyebrow lifted, and she crossed her arms. "Who's Blake?"

Audrey shook her head. "A peer from high school. He said I looked as if I could use a pick me up, and he brought me a coffee."

"Yeah, I'm sure he's just a guy from high school," her sister stated sarcastically. "Sounds like he has a soft spot for you."

"Stop it. I'm a single mom still struggling to

lose baby weight. I'm not what one might call a hot commodity." Self-esteem had never been Audrey's strongest suit. It was probably why she had fallen for Cayden's father in the first place. She had known Tony hadn't been the marrying kind, but she had let herself believe she could change him.

"You are incredible, little sis. Don't sell yourself short." Ellie patted Audrey on the shoulder before grabbing her bag. "Cayden was perfect today. He laid down for nap an hour ago. I'd stay and chat, but I promised Philip I'd make dinner tonight."

"Thanks, Sis. See you tomorrow." Audrey pushed herself off the couch to give Ellie a hug before shutting the door behind her.

As the silence descended, her mind rehashed Eliana's remarks. Could Blake be attracted to her? Or was he being nice because she was the boss's daughter? Before she could reach a conclusion, Cayden's cry pierced the air.

With a sigh, she pushed the prospect of romance from her mind and headed to Cayden's room.

udrey arrived at work the next morning eager to try out her new idea. After taking care of

Cayden the night before, her mind had wandered back to the possibility of Blake's attraction, and while she wasn't sure she was ready to date yet, she could use companionship. So, she had decided to ask him to dinner. If he declined, then he had brought the coffee to be nice. If he said yes, either he liked her or at least wanted to become better friends. It wasn't a foolproof system, but it was better than waiting and wondering.

After straightening the desk from the disarray she left it in yesterday, Audrey sat in the chair and began the task of reviewing documents for the day while keeping one eye peeled for Blake. He entered a moment later, smiling her direction.

"Morning, better day today?"

"Well, we'll see," she answered with a slight laugh. "Thank you for the coffee yesterday. It was the highlight of the day."

"You're welcome. Any time."

"Um, so I was wondering." A bout of shyness descended on Audrey, tying her tongue and forcing her eyes to the desk. "I wanted to invite you to dinner." She glanced up from lowered lids. "As a thank you."

The dimple appeared in his cheek as he returned the smile. "While no further thanks is needed, I'd love to have dinner with you. In fact, I wanted to ask you out, but you beat me to the punch."

Audrey's cheeks heated. "Sorry, I didn't mean to steal your thunder."

"I don't care who asks," Blake said, his eyes twinkling. "I'm looking forward to dinner with you."

An odd stirring sensation fluttered through Audrey's heart. "Here is the address," she said, holding out the paper she had written her address on moments earlier. "I'll make spaghetti tonight if you want to come by around seven?"

"I wouldn't miss it for the world."

The ringing phone halted any further conversation, and he flashed a wave as she picked up the handset. Though her attention should have been on the caller, she couldn't help but watch Blake exit the room.

When work ended, Audrey hurried out of the office and to the general store. Not sure if she had everything she'd need at home, she decided to just purchase all the needed ingredients. The dinner had to be perfect.

The sky outside was darkening as she parked the

car. Was it possible it might snow tonight? Audrey hoped it would hold off at least long enough for her to get home. As the chill permeated her coat, she ducked into the store and grabbed a basket. Pasta, sauce, meat, and bread found their way into her basket, and then onto the checkout conveyor belt. With the bill paid, and the groceries tucked in the front seat, she sped home.

"Can you stay a little longer tonight?" she asked Ellie as she muscled the bags into the house.

"Why? What is all this?" Ellie asked, her forehead wrinkling in confusion.

"I'm fixing dinner for Blake."

A sly smile crossed Ellie's face, and her left brow arched. "Just friends, huh?"

"It's a reciprocal gesture for yesterday," Audrey said. *And a test to see if my feelings are more than surface attraction.*

"Unh huh, a simple thank you wouldn't suffice? You had to cook the man dinner?"

Audrey set the bags on the counter and turned to her sister. "Okay, he's cute, and I'm not sure I'm ready to date yet, but it couldn't hurt to see if something's there, right?"

"Of course not, and I don't think it's too early to

date either. You said Tony left when he found out you were pregnant right?"

Audrey nodded, not wanting to correct her sister and share that Tony stayed until she gained weight and started wearing stretchy pants.

"Then I think it's time you forgot him and looked forward to the future, and this Blake sounds like a nice change. Now, go shower and clean up. I'll start the spaghetti."

"Thanks, Ellie."

Elliana nodded before shooing Audrey out of the kitchen.

After a quick shower and a change of clothes, Audrey returned to the kitchen to take over, but Cayden had woken, and Ellie shoved the bottle in her hand and ushered her to the living room instead.

Gratitude flooded Audrey. It had been hard being away from Cayden all day, and she relished holding him and watching him eat, but a small part of her felt guilty that Ellie was slaving away in the kitchen making a dinner she promised to someone else. It was spaghetti, which wasn't rocket science, but still, Ellie had her own husband to cook for.

The doorbell rang as Cayden finished his bottle. After setting it on the table, Audrey stood and opened the door for Blake who had changed as well. His dark green shirt brought out tiny tan flecks in his eyes, but it was the flowers in his hand that captured her attention. The small bouquet held six delicate orange roses, and she wondered if he understood their meaning of bridging a friendship into a romance.

"You look beautiful," he said, holding them out to her.

"Thank you. You do too. I mean handsome. You're handsome."

He smiled as she stumbled over the words. Dropping her eyes, she took the roses with her free hand and waved him inside. He followed her into the kitchen where Ellie was putting the finishing touches on dinner. "This is my sister, Elliana. She's been watching Cayden for me while I work, and she made dinner tonight."

"But only because you needed time with your son," Ellie said, jumping in and smoothing Audrey's awkward statement. "Hi, I'm Ellie," she added, sticking out her hand.

"Blake," he responded, returning the shake.

Ellie wiggled her eyebrows at Audrey in approval before turning back to the stove.

"And this is my son, Cayden," Audrey said, thankful that Blake hadn't seemed to catch Ellie's gesture. "He's the reason I'm back in town."

"He has your smile."

"And he's going to go lay down and give you guys dinner time," Ellie said as she took Cayden from Audrey's arm.

"Ellie, you don't have to. You've already been with him all day."

"Nonsense, I already checked in with Philip, and he has to work late, so I have nowhere to be. This way, I can keep him entertained and you two can have a nice dinner as adults."

Before Audrey could protest, Ellie fled with Cayden, leaving Audrey and Blake staring awkwardly at each other.

Blake broke the ice first. "Your sister is amazing."

"Yes, she is." Audrey laughed, easing the nervous tension in the room.

"And the dinner smells marvelous. It would be a shame to let it get cold, so shall we?"

"Of course, yes, let's eat." Audrey grabbed two plates from her small collection and handed him one. She scooped a portion of spaghetti and added a slice of bread to the plate in her hand and then traded plates with Blake and filled the second one. Two glasses of water sat on the table waiting for them.

"To a nice dinner with an old friend," Audrey said, raising her glass in a toast.

"To new possibilities," Blake added as he clinked her glass.

The words sent a tingle through Audrey's body. Did that mean he liked her?

"Would you mind if I prayed before we eat?"

Her daydream crashed down at his words. He was religious? She had never been one for religion herself; it held too many rules that reminded her of her overbearing mother, but as Blake was a guest in the house, she kept her opinion to herself and nodded her head. One little prayer wouldn't hurt anything, but the flames she had felt fanning inside her now smoked as if doused with water.

When he finished, an uncomfortable silence fell across the table and Audrey wondered if she should just end the date, but a voice inside her head wanted to know why.

"Why do you pray?"

The question seemed to catch Blake off guard, and he blinked at her. "You mean you don't?"

Audrey shook her head. "I was never religious. My parents never saw the need, but I tried praying in Hollywood. God didn't answer." She picked up a piece of garlic bread and took a bite.

"What were you praying for?" he asked. "If you don't mind me asking."

Audrey shrugged. "I prayed to find work, and I received enough roles to pay the rent. Then I met Tony and things improved until I got pregnant. I prayed not to be pregnant, but that one wasn't answered. When Tony left me, I prayed for work, but God didn't answer that one either."

Blake's lip folded in as if he were biting the inside of them. After a long pause, he spoke, "I'm not God, and I can't explain why it sometimes seems as if he says 'no' to our requests, but I think you might want to try praying in a different way."

Audrey's eyes flicked to his. "There's a wrong way to pray?"

"No," - he shook his head - "but a different way of praying. Jesus said we are to pray 'Thy will be done' yet many of us pray just like you did for our will to be done."

"I never knew that." Even though her words were audible, they were quiet, meant more for herself than his benefit.

Another silence descended between them, but it wasn't an uncomfortable one this time. Audrey wracked her brain for something to say when Blake sucked in his breath and pointed outside.

"Oh my goodness, it's snowing!"

Audrey whipped her head around, excitement filling her. "I love the snow, but I haven't seen it in years. LA doesn't get snow."

"Then let's go enjoy it." Blake pushed back his chair and held out his hand.

"But our dinner..."

"Will be here when we return. Come on."

With a laugh that tinkled like a bell and set her eyes sparkling, Audrey accepted his hand and the two ran to the living room to grab their coats before stepping outside.

Though chilly, the air was not biting cold yet.

"I'd forgotten how pretty it was," Audrey said with a sigh, throwing her arms out and twirling in a small circle.

"It's not as pretty as you are right now." Blake held her gaze as she paused and turned to him. A pink color tinted her lips and a tingle of embarrassment traveled through her veins.

"I'm not where I'd like to be. This baby weight is stubborn." Her eyes dropped to the ground as her self-consciousness took over.

With one large step, Blake covered the distance between them and grabbed her hands. "You are beautiful, Audrey McAllister. I've thought so since the day I first saw you in high school."

"But this isn't high school," Audrey began, glancing up at him from the corner of her eye.

"I'm glad it's not," he said with a smile. "I wouldn't have the nerve to do this if it were."

With his right hand, he tilted her face up until their eyes met. The intensity radiating from his eyes caused her to take a breath and part her lips. As if in slow motion, his head lowered until his lips gently brushed hers. The kiss was over in an instant, but the heat from his lips flamed across hers long after he had pulled back.

"I've wanted to kiss you like that for years."

"Blake, I don't know if I'm ready to jump into a relationship again," Audrey said. Though her body screamed yes, her head kept flashing a yield sign.

"That's okay, Audrey. I don't mind waiting for you. I'll wait as long as it takes."

Blake smiled as he left Audrey's house. Kissing her had been better than he'd imagined, and even though she said she wasn't ready for a relationship, he believed she was more open than she admitted.

He wanted to share his good news with someone, and he pointed his car toward The Diner. Max was locking the door as he approached.

"Well, someone looks like the cat who ate the canary," Max said, opening the door to let him in. "I guess you had a good night."

"It was amazing," Blake said, brushing the snow off his jacket.

"That's good." Max picked up the chairs, turning them upside down on the tables.

"But?" Though he hadn't said it, Blake felt the unsaid word.

"Nothing, I just don't want to see you hurt again. I don't know Audrey well, but she left once. How do you know she'll stick around this time?"

"I don't," Blake said, trying to hold on to the elated feeling he had walked in with. "I guess I'll just have to trust that God brought her back into my life for a reason."

Max shook his head. "I don't understand your faith, but for your sake, I'll hope so too."

CHAPTER 7

*W*hen Friday night rolled around, Audrey clocked out right at five o'clock and headed to the parking lot. The last few days, she had been waiting to walk out with Blake, but tonight was her dinner with her parents and she couldn't be late.

"Oh good, you're back. Mother called and said Philip and I have to attend this dinner too, so I have to run home and change," Elliana said as Audrey entered the house.

"Ellie, I'm sorry. Is she requesting you attend once a month like me or just this once?"

"I'm not sure. I hope it's just this once, but now my nerves are all bunched up. Why does she always make me feel like I've been called to the principal's office when she makes me come over?"

Audrey smiled as she took Cayden from her sister's arms. "I feel the same way." She turned her attention to the baby. "How are you, little man?"

"Cayden was an angel today. I wonder how Mother will deal with a baby."

"Is it awful that I kind of hope he throws a fit and makes a big enough mess that she won't make us come back?"

"I don't think so," Ellie said with a laugh. "I'd have the same thoughts. Okay, I have to run and change, but I'll see you there."

Ellie's car wasn't at the mansion when Audrey arrived. She stifled the sigh threatening to escape. Seeing her mother again would be a lot easier with Ellie to act as mediator. A check of the clock revealed only a few minutes before seven, so surely she would arrive soon.

After turning off the engine, Audrey grabbed Cayden's car seat from the back and drug her feet up the walkway to the front door. It was just dinner, so why did it feel like impending doom?

Julie answered the door before the bell had finished ringing. "She's waiting for you in the dining room," she said in a clipped tone. Audrey knew she had been cutting it close, but she wasn't late, unless her watch was off.

Audrey followed Julie into the spacious dining room decorated in creams and golds to make it appear more opulent. A large table filled the middle of the room though Audrey could never remember having people at dinner.

Her father, Bruce, sat at the head of the table, a newspaper open in his hands. Though he had the money to buy whatever technology he wanted, he had never given up the paper newspaper, claiming reading it online just wasn't the same.

"Ah, finally. I thought perhaps you were breaking our deal," Evelyn said, rising from the chair next to her father. "Please come sit down and join us so we can eat before the food is ice cold."

"I'm not late, Mother. My clock said it was 6:57 when I pulled in." Audrey worked hard to keep the irritation out of her voice.

With an exaggerated gesture, Evelyn glanced at the diamond encrusted watch on her wrist and pursed her lips. "Perhaps it is time you obtain a new watch. Mine shows ten after seven, and I highly doubt you took ten minutes to get here from the atrium."

This would be harder than Audrey thought. Where was her sister to help out? After placing Cayden's carrier on the floor next to her father, Audrey pulled out the chair across from her mother and sat down. "Are we waiting for Ellie?"

"Elliana called and said Philip is sick, so they will not be making it tonight."

Dread settled in Audrey's stomach.

"Ah, Audrey," her father said, lowering his newspaper. "Good to see you again. How are you enjoying work?"

"The position is challenging to be sure, but I think I'm getting a better hang on it."

"Good, good."

"Can we eat now?" The vein of contempt was ripe in Evelyn's voice

"Of course." Bruce folded his newspaper and placed it under the plate.

Evelyn picked up the dainty silver bell at the end of the table and rang it. Audrey closed her eyes and took a deep breath. How did her parents justify this? They didn't need anyone to wait on them hand and foot.

Julie appeared a moment later pushing a cart laden with small china bowls. Without a word, she placed one before Evelyn, Bruce, and Audrey and then stepped back and waited.

"Thank you, Julie, that will be all," Evelyn said, and Julie curtsied and left.

Not thinking, Audrey lowered her head and closed her eyes. After their dinner on Tuesday, she and Blake had eaten lunch together the rest of the week, and though she still wasn't sure she was ready to be religious, she had shown respect and bowed her head each time.

"What are you doing?" Evelyn asked.

Audrey's head popped up, a faint heat searing across her cheeks. "Sorry, I've been seeing Blake Dalton, and he prays before every meal. Bowing my head was just habit."

"Blake Dalton," her father said, rubbing his chin, "why does that name sound familiar?"

"Because he works for you Dad. He's on the construction crew." Audrey shook her head, wondering how he could not know one of his own employees.

"You've been seeing one of your father's employees?" Evelyn asked.

"Well, we only had one real date, but we've been having lunch together. I like him. He's nice."

"You can't keep seeing him," her mother said,

lowering her head and dipping her spoon into the bowl as if the discussion were over.

"What do you mean I can't keep seeing him?" White hot anger bubbled in Audrey's stomach. "I'm a grown woman. You can't tell me who I can and can't see."

"Maybe not, but you are a McAllister. We marry higher than common construction workers."

The anger grew so intense that red flashed across Audrey's eyes. "That is horrible, Mother. Just because he's a construction worker doesn't make him less of a person. And no one said anything about marriage. I'm not ready to marry. We had one date for goodness sakes." It took all of Audrey's strength to keep her voice even as Cayden was sleeping in the carrier beside her, and she didn't want to wake him. "Dad, tell her that Blake is a good guy."

While Bruce rarely stood up to Evelyn, he was more level headed and not as obsessed with status. "Blake is a good guy, but..."

"I can't believe you two. This is the reason I moved away to LA," she said emphasizing each word. "I didn't want to end up like you guys, so obsessed with money."

"Why can't you find someone like Phillip?" Her mother asked.

"Stop it. You've always compared me to Elliana. I was never smart enough or pretty enough for you. Now I can't even date the right guy? You know what? Fire me if you want. I'll pay back what I borrowed as soon as I can, but I'm going to keep seeing Blake."

Evelyn's mouth dropped open, but before she could say anything, Audrey leaned down and grabbed Cayden's carrier. "I'll show myself out."

Her anger didn't fade as she stomped out of the front door and climbed into her car though as she closed the door, the fear set in.

If she lost her job, how would she pay her rent? Without thinking, words spilled out of her mouth in a prayer.

"Lord, I don't know what to do without help. Please show me what to do."

CHAPTER 8

"*W*hat's the matter?" Blake asked as Audrey opened the door Sunday morning.

Audrey shook her head. "It was a rough weekend. When I came to town, I had no money, so I had to ask my parents for help. They agreed, but only if I worked for my father and attended a dinner with them once a month. Friday was the first dinner and needless to say, it didn't go well."

"I'm sorry," he said, touching her arm. "What happened?"

She bit her lip as she glanced up at him, wondering if she should tell him. She didn't want to hurt him, but if they were going to have a relationship—and she thought that's where they were heading—then she wanted to share everything with him. "My parents forbade me from seeing you because you don't meet their idea of what I should be dating. I left, but not before telling them I didn't need their money, but in reality, I do."

The news that her parents didn't approve of Blake didn't appear to faze him in the least. Instead, he opened his arms and Audrey stepped into them, enjoying the warmth and security they provided. "It will be okay," he said, patting her hair. The simple touch felt like home, and she buried her face further in his chest.

"How? I even prayed on the way home, but I haven't had any bright idea come to me." Her voice was muffled against his shirt, but he seemed to understand her anyway.

"We'll figure something out."

Audrey pulled back and looked up at him. "Unless it's the fact that you're a secret millionaire, I doubt it will change their mind."

Blake said nothing, but a small smile pulled at the corner of his mouth.

Audrey's eyes narrowed at him. "Are you a secret millionaire?"

"Maybe not a millionaire," Blake laughed, "but I do have quite a bit of money to my name."

"But, if you have so much money, why are you working for my father?"

Blake brushed a strand of her blond hair back behind her ear. "I work because I like it, and because I don't want to end up one of those people who becomes attached to money and looks down on everyone else."

Audrey snorted. "It's like you've met my mother."

"I have," - Blake said - "at the Christmas party last year, but I don't think your mother is bad. She's just missing something in her life."

"What?" Audrey asked, her brow furrowing. Her mother was lacking for nothing except for maybe decent civility.

"God. All the money in the world means nothing if I don't have two things—God being the first."

"What's the second?"

Blake's hazel eyes stared into hers. "Love," he said as his thumb caressed her cheek. "First Corinthians says, 'three things will last forever—faith, hope, and love—and the greatest of these is love.' But if you don't have Jesus in your heart, it's hard to understand love."

Suddenly, Audrey wanted to know Jesus the way Blake seemed to. She wanted the peace he exuded. "Will you teach me about love?"

There was a double meaning in her words, and Blake didn't miss it. His eyes glistened as he nodded. "I would love to teach you about love." Then his eyes closed, and his head lowered to hers, sending a tremor of emotion through her body as his lips pressed against hers. Her hands wound around his neck, her fingers locking in his hair. As his hands lowered to her low back, he pulled her closer to him and the kiss deepened until the cry from Cayden broke them apart.

"I think he might be jealous," Blake said, brushing a finger across Audrey's lips. "But we need to get going anyway or we won't make it to church."

Audrey nodded. Any words she might have been able to respond with had left her head when his lips seared hers.

Ten minutes later, they were pulling into the parking lot of the small white church. A large white steeple that held a bell rose from the left side of the building and a single cross sat in the middle of the roof. Stained glass windows dotted the building, adding bursts of color to the plain white siding.

Blake grabbed Cayden's car seat from the back and slung it over his left arm, leaving his right hand free to clasp Audrey's hand. When his fingers entwined with hers, she couldn't stop the smile that spread across her face.

"Hello, Blake, good to see you." A young man with dark hair and a bright smile greeted them as they approached the entrance.

"Hello, Pastor Tom. It's good to see you again too. Are you teaching today?"

"Yes sir. Pastor Robert is taking a few weeks off."

"This is my friend Audrey McAllister. Audrey, this is Pastor Tom."

Tom's eyes widened at the name, and Audrey smirked. "Yep, Bruce McAllister is my father. I'm sort of the black sheep of the family I guess."

"Well, sheep of all color are welcome here," Tom said with a laugh. "We will have to try to get your parents to join us."

Audrey rolled her eyes. "Good luck with that. Religion isn't their thing."

"But it wasn't yours either, remember?" Blake said, squeezing her hand.

"That's true, but I think I was an easier sell than they will be."

"We'll keep praying regardless," Tom said. "And we're glad to have you here today."

Audrey followed Blake into the sanctuary, feeling out of her element. She couldn't remember the last time she had been in a church. Rows of chairs filled the open room, and a stage at the front held a piano, a drum set, and a few guitars. One large white screen hung on the wall at the very back of the stage.

As Cayden was awake, Audrey rescued him from the carrier after they sat down and held him on her lap. His eyes flicked back and forth as if taking the new environment in.

The room filled quickly, and those who knew Blake came by and greeted him. Blake was careful to introduce her each time, but she knew she would never remember all the names. Perhaps after she had been coming a few weeks, they would stick in her memory. She paused at that thought. She had never planned to stay when she came home, but the idea didn't sound so bad now.

When the music started, Audrey found herself swaying to the beat, though she didn't know most of the words. Blake sang beside her, his voice a clear, strong tenor. She'd had no idea he could sing, but she found she wouldn't mind hearing his voice every Sunday.

After the songs ended, Pastor Tom took the stage. Audrey had no Bible, but Blake held his out, so they could look at it together. When the words 'but the greatest of these is love' hit her ears, Audrey glanced up. Was it just an odd coincidence that the pastor was speaking on the very verse Blake had said to her this morning or was this God speaking to her? She turned to Blake, who smiled and nodded at her.

As the pastor continued to speak, Audrey's heart called out to God asking him to lead her, to change her, and to show her love.

When the service ended, Blake took her to The Diner for lunch. It appeared to be the hangout place after church on Sunday as several other church goers ended up there as well. Audrey was glad Blake didn't call them over or ask them to join their table though. It wasn't that she didn't want to get to know everyone soon, but she wanted a little time with Blake to decompress and discuss his plan for the next day.

"I'm so glad I got to know you," Audrey said as they opened the menus. "I know it hasn't been long, but I feel like a different person now."

"Well, it's been a lot longer for me," Blake said with a smile. "I've been waiting to be with you for years."

Heat climbed up Audrey's face at the compliment. She couldn't believe this wonderful man had been in front of her all those years ago and she had been too blind to see it.

"But you are a different person now. Accepting

God into your heart changes you. Now we just need to get your parents and your sister together, so we can see about changing their hearts too."

"Do you think it will work?" Audrey asked. "I can't see my mother ever giving up her money and leaning on Jesus."

"Well, she doesn't necessarily have to give up her money, but as for leaning on Jesus, I've seen tougher cases than your mother come around. Never doubt what God can do. Christmas is next week, and that seems to help with people's spirits too. We'll figure something out."

Audrey nodded, but the doubt still rumbled around in her head. She wanted him to be right. No, she needed him to be right, but it would take a miracle to turn her mother around.

CHAPTER 9

*A*udrey applied the last dab of lipstick and leaned forward to inspect the finished product in the mirror. Not bad, if she did say so herself.

When the knock sounded at the door, her heart fluttered in her chest. She hadn't expected to fall for someone in Star Lake and certainly not so fast.

With a smile, she flung the door open to greet Blake, but it wasn't Blake who stared back at her from the front stoop.

"Tony? What are you doing here?" On the other side stood the man she thought she'd never see again, the dark-haired Italian who had left her six months ago.

"I came for you and my son. Audrey, I'm sorry I wasn't there. I should have been."

"How did you even find me?" Confusion covered Audrey, clouding her thoughts. She and Tony had never spoken of her hometown; he had never appeared interested.

"Dez told me you came home for money. I had no idea you were from such a small town, but once I arrived, it was easy to follow the gossip train to your house. You don't have to stay any longer. Return to LA with me and let's create a life together."

Audrey opened her mouth to say no, but indecision flooded her. She wanted to go back to LA, didn't she? It's what she had told herself when she first moved back, but now Blake was in the picture, and she was no longer sure.

"I'm not positive I want to go back. I mean I want to act again but there's something magical about this town."

Tony blinked at her. "This town? This town has one stoplight and no Starbucks. Why would you live in the middle of nowhere when you aren't forced to?"

Audrey shrugged. "I don't know. There's something about the small-town vibe I like. It's kind of growing on me again."

Cayden's cry interrupted the discussion and Audrey turned to get him.

"Is that him? I want to see him." Tony followed her into the house and to Cayden's room.

As Audrey picked Cayden up out of the crib, Tony reached for him. "Please, let me hold my son."

After a moment's hesitation, Audrey held the bundle out, adjusting his arms the way the nurse had showed her that first day in the hospital. Though sweet, the image triggered the memory that Tony hadn't been there, that he had left her when she started gaining weight to have the baby alone.

"I need to get his bottle. Can you hold him without dropping him?"

"I think I can manage," Tony said with a narrowed look.

Audrey wasn't so sure, but she exited the room anyway. She filled the bottle quickly and returned, afraid to leave Cayden too long. "Here let me take him," she said, holding out her arms.

"I can feed him. Just hand over the bottle."

Audrey bit her lip, but before she could argue, a knock sounded at the door. *Blake. Oh no, this will not be good.*

"Who's that?" Tony's eyes shifted to the door and he moved that direction.

"A friend of mine," Audrey said. "I'll get the door. You sit in the chair and feed Cayden."

With heavy feet, Audrey walked to the door, playing different scenarios over in her head. She could tell Blake Tony was here, but how would he react? The other option involved lying, which brought a different kind of unease and Blake would see right through the lie and want an explanation.

"Evening," he said, as the door opened.

"Hi." He leaned in for a kiss, but she placed a hand on his chest, stopping the motion. "Um, Tony's here."

Blake's face blanked for a moment as if trying to place the name, and then he nodded, but his face remained devoid of emotion.

Audrey hated hurting him. "I didn't invite him," she continued hoping to ease the evident tension in the air. "He found out where I lived from my old roommate and just showed up. I wanted to throw him out, but Cayden is his son."

"I understand. Do you want me to stay?" His voice held no emotion and tugged at Audrey's heartstrings.

Though she wanted him to stay, with no idea what Tony would do, she worried his staying would make the situation worse. "Can we take a rain check and talk at work tomorrow?"

Blake took a deep breath and nodded, sadness

manifesting across his handsome features. "Okay, I'll talk to you tomorrow."

Audrey couldn't let him leave without trying to make him understand her conundrum, but as she reached out to touch his arm, Tony's voice sounded from behind her. "Who is this?"

"This is my friend Blake. We had planned to hang out tonight before you showed up." Audrey fought to keep her voice calm. Cayden was still in Tony's arms, and fear at what he might do if challenged coursed through her veins.

"Well, I'm in town now to take care of Audrey and Cayden, so thanks for stopping by Brad, but..."

"Blake. The name is Blake." Blake's shoulders tensed as his eyes narrowed.

Audrey took a step toward Tony, hoping to extricate Cayden from his arms in case blows were about to rain down.

"Whatever. We're good, so you can leave."

Audrey reached out for Cayden, but Tony turned away, clutching the baby in his large hands.

Blake's eyes flashed. "I'll leave, but only because Audrey asked, and I'll be checking in with her again."

As the door closed behind Blake, the anger bubbling in Audrey rose to the surface. "That was rude, Tony. Blake is a friend."

"Looks like he wants to be more than friends."

"Maybe he does. Maybe I do. After all, you left me when I was five months pregnant because I gained too much weight. He knows I have a kid, and he doesn't care about my weight."

"I'm sorry I left, Audrey. I wasn't sure I could be a dad, but, I want my son in my life." Tony crossed to the couch and sat down, still cradling Cayden in the crook of his arm.

Audrey crossed her arms, angry at Tony's leaving and then showing up unannounced, but the ire fizzled the longer she watched him. Tony held Cayden and gazed at him as if he wanted to be a father. How often had she dreamed about him coming back and raising their son with her? And shouldn't she want Cayden to be around his real father? But then there was Blake. Audrey felt closer to Blake in one week than she could remember being to Tony the whole time they had been together. Audrey sighed as she sat in the chair across from him. What was she going to do now?

The snow crunched under Blake's feet on the journey back to his truck. This was an unexpected turn of events. Not only was he having to overcome Audrey's parents' objection to him, but now Cayden's father was in the picture.

Max was busy behind the counter when Blake stepped into The Diner. He chose the last empty seat at the counter, next to Bert.

"Hello, Blake. Where is your pretty friend tonight?" Bert asked, closing his book and turning his attention on Blake.

Blake shook his head, not wanting to drudge through the issue with Bert, whom he rarely spoke to. "Something came up."

Max, overhearing the exchange, shot Blake a questioning look.

"Just a burger for now," Blake said, knowing Max would want the full story later.

Max nodded and put the order in, and when the burger arrived, Blake tried to eat it, but couldn't muster the desire to finish it.

An hour later, the last customer left. After locking the door and flipping the sign to 'Closed,' Max walked back to the counter and sat next to Blake.

"Okay, spill it. What's going on?"

A long, deep sigh spilled out. "We were supposed to meet tonight and brainstorm ways to smooth the issue with her parents, but when I got there, Tony was there."

Max's brow furrowed. "Who's Tony again?"

"Cayden's father. Evidently he just showed up unannounced, and she seemed unsure of what to do. I think I love her, but I don't want to keep a child from his father. I don't know what to do." Blake dropped his head into his hands.

Max clapped a hand on his shoulder. "Hey, I know I'm not as religious as you, but don't you always say God knows best? I think the best thing you can do is wait. Let her know you're there, but wait and see what happens."

Blake raised his head to regard his friend. "I wasn't sure you had been listening, but I'm glad some of my advice wore off on you. It's nice to hear it back, but it doesn't make it any easier to follow."

"It never does, my friend," Max said.

CHAPTER 10

"How long do you plan on staying, Tony?" Audrey asked as she cleaned the dinner dishes. After Blake's exit, Audrey had whipped up dinner hoping Tony would eat and leave, but he appeared in no hurry to leave.

"Leave? I'm not leaving. This is my son, and I'm taking you both back to California."

Audrey sighed and turned off the water. "Tony, you didn't understand. I'm not going back. I'm enjoying being home."

A sneer crossed Tony's face as he stood and closed the distance between them. "Are you sure you're not enjoying your new boyfriend?"

Audrey stepped back as fear flooded her body. Tony had never been violent, but she didn't like the vibe he was emitting. "It's not like that. Blake is a

Christian who hasn't pressured me to do anything, unlike someone else from my past."

While Audrey had been interested in Tony, things had moved at a faster pace because Tony had pushed. Perhaps if Audrey had been stronger, she would have noticed some of the less desirable traits Tony possessed, and run instead of jumping into bed with him.

"I never had to pressure you," Tony said with a sadistic laugh. "You would have done anything to get ahead and land a starring role."

Anger replaced the fear as the realization he had never cared for her sunk in. "You took advantage of me."

Tony snorted. "It's Hollywood, baby, what did you expect? You do what you must to get ahead and succeed. If you plan to make it there, you better learn that lesson."

"Then I guess it's good I don't plan on going back." The words surprised even Audrey as they exited her mouth. She had planned on returning one day, when the money grew, and Cayden was a little older, but seeing Tony now opened her eyes. Audrey reflected on the other things done to get roles and cringed. A tiny ember of self-loathing flickered within her.

Tony's voice softened. "Look, Audrey, let's sleep on it. You'll change your mind in the morning after I've reminded you how much fun we have."

Audrey shook her head in repulsion. How had she fallen for this hardened, insensitive man? Had fame been so blinding she had convinced herself of his charm? "I'm not spending the night with you, and you're not staying here. Go home, Tony. I don't know why you're really here, but you don't want to be a father."

"You have no idea what I want," Tony said, narrowing his eyes. "I'll leave tonight, but this isn't over."

When the door shut, Audrey rushed to lock it before sinking to the carpet, her back against the door. "Lord, I don't know what to do. Help me get Tony out of my life."

Audrey filled Elliana in on the previous night's events when she arrived the following morning.

"Should I worry this guy will show up here?" Fear threaded Elliana's normally bold voice.

"I don't expect he will, but I honestly have no

idea. If he does, call me and then drive to Mother's. If anything can scare him away, Evelyn might be it."

The girls exchanged tentative smiles laced with apprehension. Audrey didn't want to leave Cayden, and she hated placing Elliana in an awkward situation, but she had to get to work.

Blake was waiting at the front desk when she arrived. "I wanted to check and make sure everything was okay."

His words, meant to uplift, only reinforced the fear, and she began shaking. "I'm not sure if it will be okay. Tony left last night, but says he won't go back to California without Cayden. Elliana is home with Cayden now, but what if Tony returns?"

"Have Elliana take Cayden somewhere safe. Maybe to your mother's?"

Audrey nodded. "I told her to go there if Tony showed up."

"No, now, before Tony shows up. At least that way Evelyn is there to help, and she's forceful enough to be convincing. I will call Sergeant Powell and see if there's any information on Tony's past we can use as leverage."

Blake's words sent Audrey's head spinning, and she gaped at him unsure of where to start.

"What's Tony's last name?"

"Bachetti," Audrey managed through the cloud of uncertainty.

"Good, call Elliana. I'll be right back." Blake's tone was firm and pushed Audrey into gear.

She picked up the desk phone as he pulled out his cell.

Within minutes, Blake and Audrey were in his car on the way to her house. Audrey clutched a fax in her hand, surprised at the information it contained. She'd had no idea Tony had a record, but hoped it would be enough to get him to leave.

Tony's car was in the driveway when they pulled up, but thankfully Ellie's wasn't.

"You ready?" Blake asked, squeezing her hand after turning off the engine.

Audrey nodded, though her nerves were wound as tight as a drum. After a final deep breath, she opened the car door and stepped out.

"Where's my son?" Tony asked approaching her. An aggressive wave rolled off his demeanor halting Audrey's steps until Blake's hand landed on her back, a reassuring gesture.

"Cayden's not here," Audrey said after flashing a look of gratitude Blake's direction. "You didn't come here seeking to be Cayden's father. You came here in hopes of money, but you won't get any."

"What are you talking about?"

"This!" Audrey held out the paper and Tony snatched it, his eyes widening at the information. "You shouldn't even be here, Tony. According to this, you are violating parole, and I'm sure the LAPD would love to obtain that information."

Tony's eyes narrowed into slits.

"Or you can go back to LA and forget about Audrey and Cayden and we can tear this paper up," Blake said, taking a step forward.

"You haven't seen the last of me." Tony scowled before crumpling the paper and stomping to his car.

As the black Mercedes Benz roared to life, and the tires squealed out of the driveway, Audrey sagged against Blake, the adrenaline leaving her knees weak.

"Everything will be okay," Blake said, wrapping both arms around her. "We'll get a lawyer and get you full custody, so he can't do this again."

Audrey turned to Blake. "Thank you. I couldn't have done this without you."

Instead of a verbal response, his arms tightened

around her, and he lowered his head to mark her lips with his own.

"I want to make sure Cayden's okay," Audrey said as the kiss ended. The desire to remain in Blake's chiseled arms was strong, but so was the maternal instinct to check on her son. Blake nodded and ten minutes later they pulled into the estate.

Elliana opened the door instead of Julie, sending alarm bells ringing in Audrey's head.

"Where's Cayden? Is he okay?" Audrey asked. Her eyes darted behind Elliana in search of her son.

"Relax, he's fine. He's with Mother. Tony never even showed up here."

"That's because we met him first. I hope he won't be back," Audrey said.

"If he does, we'll figure something out," Blake said, squeezing her shoulder.

"I need to see Cayden."

Ellie led the way to the formal living room where Evelyn sat with Cayden on her lap.

The change in Evelyn stopped Audrey in her tracks. Not only was Evelyn not in a pantsuit, but no pearls adorned her neck. "Mother?"

Evelyn looked up and smiled, sending another shock of disbelief down Audrey's spine. When was the last time her mother had smiled like that?

"Ah, Audrey, Blake, welcome."

Audrey glanced at Blake who shrugged and then she turned her attention to Ellie. With a raise of her eyebrows, she asked the silent question, knowing Ellie would understand.

"You got me," Ellie said with a laugh. "She's been like this for about an hour. After Cayden spit up on her white Nina McLemore suit, she changed into this and her whole attitude shifted. You should have seen her laying on the floor with him."

"I can relax on occasion," Evelyn said, feigning mock hurt.

"No, you can't Mother," Audrey said. She wanted to scoop up Cayden to make sure he was okay, but shock kept her rooted in place.

"Ah, Blake," her father's voice grabbed everyone's attention as he entered the living room, "I want to say thank you for your calm head today."

"You're welcome, Sir. I'm glad I could help."

"You should all stay for dinner," Evelyn said, "though with all the hubbub today, I'm not sure Maurice cooked anything, but there is always pizza."

"Pizza? Mother are you feeling all right?" Audrey moved to a chair and sat down, the complete and utter change in Evelyn too much to deal with.

Evelyn shot a pointed look and sighed. "I'm fine.

Look, when I heard Tony was trying to take Cayden away, I realized more important things in life exist than money, but if you'd like me to go back..."

"No," Audrey and Ellie shouted simultaneously and then laughed. "No, Mother," Audrey said, "We like this new you. It's just going to take some getting used to, but I hope you've also changed your mind about Blake." She smiled up at him and reached for his hand. "Because I expect he will be in my life for the foreseeable future." He squeezed her hand and grinned.

"I think we may have been too hasty in our earlier judgment," Bruce said, clearing his throat. "Anyone who can conduct himself the way Blake did today is welcome in my house and to date my daughter."

"Thank you, Bruce, and while I don't think it matters, I can support Audrey financially. My father was very wealthy, and when he died, he left me a small fortune.

"I'm glad to hear it, but I agree with Evelyn. Money has been our bane for far too long. Family is what really matters."

Audrey and Ellie shared another glance, and Audrey knew Ellie was wondering the same thing: Was this for real and would it last?

"I think you should stay here," Evelyn said as the family retired into the living room after dinner. "At least until we know Tony has left town."

Audrey shook her head. "I can't, Mother. All of Cayden's stuff is at my house. I need to go back."

"Evelyn might be right," Blake said. "I'm not comfortable with you staying there alone either," he raised his hand as Audrey opened her mouth to object, "but I know you need to be at home, so I was wondering if anyone would object to my staying on her couch at least for tonight."

"I could agree to that," Evelyn said. "It sounds like you proved yourself today."

"I can't say I'm a fan of you two being in the house alone together," Bruce said.

"I understand your concern Bruce," Blake said. "But I'm a God-fearing man. While I care for your daughter, my love for God is even greater. I assure you I will do nothing to harm that relationship or your daughter's virtue."

Bruce leaned back and regarded Blake. "I don't know about this God thing, but not many men today would say what you did, so I will accept it as well."

A handshake sealed the deal, and after a round of

hugs—another thing that never happened in the McAllister household—Audrey and Blake headed out to the car.

"That might just have been the weirdest day of my life," Audrey said as Blake strapped Cayden in the car seat.

"I thought it was nice," Blake said.

"No, it was nice," Audrey said as she buckled her seatbelt. "But you met my mother before. Is it natural for someone to make such a drastic change in so short a time?"

Blake smiled. "I'm no expert, but the threat of loss can cause drastic changes. Couple that with the fact we've been praying for them, and I'm not surprised at all."

"I hope you're right. They invited us over for Christmas on Friday. Feel up to it?"

He squeezed her hand before starting the car and turning his attention to the road. "I wouldn't miss it for the world. Do you think they would mind if I brought my mother?"

Audrey chuckled and shook her head. "Yesterday, I wouldn't have even believed they would invite you, but after tonight, I don't think they'd mind."

udrey glanced around the room and marveled at the difference. Years ago, when she left, she would never have pictured a happy gathering at her parent's house.

Blake had told her the Christmas party was often held at work, but Evelyn had hired a last-minute decorator to adorn the house, so it would exude a welcoming and Christmassy air for the party. No expense had been spared. A twelve-foot tree complete with lights and decorations sat near the fireplace and twinkle lights hung from the beams in the ceiling. Garland draped across nearly every surface and fake snowflakes hung from invisible threads.

Even more surprising was that half the town had showed up at the McAllister's invite. Max and Layla stood by the long table sipping eggnog or cider. Bert and Amelia sat on one of the white couches looking like uncomfortable statues afraid to touch anything. Only their eyes moved back and forth as they watched the crowd. Paula had cornered Barnard near the tree and the two were arguing over whether white lights or colored lights looked better on trees.

Evelyn and Bruce sat in the chairs nearest the fireplace with Cayden asleep on Evelyn's lap. She had scooped him up as soon as Audrey arrived and carried him around the room showing him off to everyone. Audrey couldn't remember seeing her mother so happy.

Blake's mother, Irene, stood near Evelyn smiling down at Cayden's dark head. She had spent most of the night by Evelyn's side, probably to be by the baby, but now the two appeared to be fast friends. Audrey shook her head at the image. She would never have believed it if she wasn't seeing it with her own eyes.

Last but certainly not least, Philip and Elliana stood near the refreshments sharing a quiet conversation. Audrey smiled as she watched Elliana touch Philip's arm and laugh. It was obvious her sister was still very much in love with her husband.

"Come here." Blake grabbed Audrey's hand and pulled her out of the living room.

"Where are we going?" Audrey asked, laughing.

"I want a moment alone with you," Blake said. His eyes scanned the doorways as he pulled her from one room to another. "Ah, there we go."

Audrey looked up and felt the heat sear across her face. Hanging from the door jamb was a bright green sprig of mistletoe.

"You needed a mistletoe to kiss me?" Audrey laughed.

"No, but it makes it more romantic at Christmastime, don't you think?" His arms circled her waist as he pulled her closer.

Her arms wound around his neck, and she smiled. "I can't imagine anything more romantic." As she closed her eyes, her lips parted expecting his, but nothing came. She opened her eyes, confused.

Blake's grin reached from ear to ear. "I wanted to tell you before I kissed you that I had one thing even more romantic than Mistletoe."

Audrey couldn't imagine anything more romantic than being under the mistletoe with Blake. "What's that?"

"I heard from the LA police today. Tony was back at work today, so you can relax and enjoy the holiday. I asked a friend of mine to keep a tab on him and let me know if he disappears again."

"That may be the best Christmas present ever,"

Audrey said with a smile. Though she'd miss having Blake on her couch, she was relieved she could stop worrying about Tony showing up and stealing Cayden in the night.

"No, the best Christmas present ever is you," Blake said. "I love you Audrey McAllister."

"I love you too, Blake Dalton."

Electricity crackled between them as he lowered his face to hers. When his lips touched hers, heat flooded her body. She couldn't believe how much her life had changed in such a short time, but she wouldn't trade it for the world.

The End!

LOVE CONQUERS ALL PREVIEW

If you loved Once Upon a Star, be sure to look for Love Conquers All, coming soon.

Lanie Hall's footsteps echoed in the now half empty house. True to his word, Denny had cleared out his half of the furniture. The rusty orange recliner she had always hated? Gone. The glass topped coffee table she had always imagined children breaking and cutting themselves on? It was gone too. The fact they had never had kids to break the coffee table hadn't deterred her fears over the years.

All that remained of the living room furniture now was the couch her parents had given her when she first moved out. Faded and slightly stained, but otherwise in decent shape, it had lasted through college, and without kids, had held up well over the years as well.

Lanie wandered into the kitchen. Most of the appliances remained on the counter, but she did note the absence of the coffee pot. She might have to replace that as Denny's morning coffee habit had rubbed off on her some time in their ten years together.

With a heavy heart, Lanie followed the hallway into the bedroom which had felt empty for the last few years anyway. Somewhere around their fifth year of marriage, she and Denny had stopped touching and kissing. Forget sleeping in the same room at the same time. She would turn in and read a new book or get lost in a tv show until she fell asleep. He would fall asleep in the living room and leave for work without even saying goodbye. And that's how the last few years had passed.

Lanie crossed to the closet and opened the door. The small room had once been bursting with both their clothes, but now only hers hung on one side, creating a haphazard effect like a sinking ship. With a sigh she thought back to the last conversation she'd had with Denny.

"I can't do this anymore, Lanie. We hardly talk, and when we do, it's short and curt. I want to experience something again."

"Let's try counseling, Denny," Lanie said, curling her hands against her legs. "I don't like feeling like roommates either."

"We could." Denny nodded and ran a hand through his short brown hair, "but I don't expect it would help. Neither of us is getting anything out of this marriage any longer. I think it best we go our separate ways."

Lanie blinked at him but nodded. A part of her had hoped he would fight, that he would agree to counseling or something else, but his adamant stance informed her he no longer cared to try. It saddened her a little, but she didn't have the energy to fight for them both.

She shut the closet door, hating the reminder of her failed marriage. Though the divorce wasn't official yet, it was only a matter of time. Denny was gone, and the paperwork was filed. As they hadn't wanted any of the same things and they planned on selling the house and splitting the profits, the smooth process had taken no time, and now she was simply playing the waiting game.

Suddenly, the house felt too empty, too condemning, and Lanie needed a break. She retraced her steps, grabbing her keys at the door, and hurried to her car. With no idea of where to go, she let her mind wander and her hands do the steering, but it wasn't much of a surprise when she pulled into Mic's, the radio station hang out.

It had been where she had spent many Friday nights, belting out karaoke until Denny decided he no longer wanted to go out. He had never insisted she not go, but there had been a silent request coupled with a heaping of guilt, and she had eventually stopped showing up.

Lanie paused with her hand on the door handle. What if this was no longer the hangout? What if she stepped inside and recognized no one there. Squaring her shoulders, she decided she didn't care. It couldn't be any worse or feel any lonelier than her empty house.

The darkened club looked exactly as she remembered if a little emptier, but a check of her wristwatch revealed the hour was still early. She sidled up to the bar for a drink, not because she was much of a drinker, but because she needed something to do.

"What'll you have?" the bartender asked. His bald pate contrasted with a full, thick beard, which formed an interesting contrast. Large gages created gaping holes in his ears, but his kind smile softened the hard image.

"Can I have a sprite please?"

The bartender raised one eyebrow at her, but turned and grabbed a glass.

"Lanie? Lanie Hall?"

Lanie looked to the left where the voice had come from, and her breath caught. Azarius Jacobson, a blast from her past, stood there dapper as ever in grey jeans and a darker grey shirt that accentuated his finely-toned arms.

They had once worked together at the radio station, though he had quit and done something else shortly after her marriage to Denny.

"Azarius? How have you been?" she asked before throwing her arms around him. They hadn't been close when he worked at the station years ago, but he was a familiar face on a day she needed one.

He chuckled as her weight knocked him a step backwards, and his arms surrounded her to keep them both from falling over.

Though purely innocent, she hadn't had a man's arms around her in so long that it ignited a flame deep inside her, and a heated flush crawled up her face as she registered his touch. "Sorry, I'm just excited to see someone I know, and I haven't seen you for what? Six years?"

"Eight," he said, dropping his arms. "You look fantastic. Just as I remembered."

Just as he remembered? The flush climbed higher up her face. She had only a vague memory of him from when he worked at the radio station, but he appeared to have a much better memory of her.

"You look great too. Why don't you get a drink and join me? I'd love to hear what you've been up to." Why did the simple thought of him joining her send her heart racing?

"Sure, I'd love to catch up with you."

He ordered a Vodka Tonic and led the way to an empty table.

"When did you get back to town?" she asked as they sat. The light above bounced off his dark skin, creating a glittering caramel effect.

"About six months ago," he said. "I'm not working for the radio station this time though."

She smiled as she sipped her soda. "I figured you weren't. I'm still there, and I would have noticed if you were back."

"Would you have?" His dark brown eyes bored into her soul, and she dropped her eyes and bit her lip.

"Honestly, I don't know," she said, stirring her straw in a circle. "Things have been crazy."

"Oh yeah? What's been going on?"

His gaze never wavered from her, and the intensity of it sent a shiver down her spine. When was the last time someone had looked at her like that? As if he really saw her? Years, she decided. It had been years, and the simple act not only made her feel beautiful but lowered her emotional walls.

"My marriage fell apart," she sighed. "I guess it had been going that direction for awhile, but we finally decided to stop fighting the lack of feelings and call it quits."

"I'm sorry to hear that," he said, but something about his expression made her wonder if he really were sorry.

"So, what about you?" she asked, changing the subject. Her failed marriage was a topic she wanted to forget, not rehash. "How has life been for you?"

He shrugged. "It's been. I re-enlisted for awhile. You knew I was National Guard, right?"

Lanie blinked and shook her head. She'd had no idea he was in the service. Wow, she really had been clueless about him. That was a pretty big piece of information to miss about someone.

"Oh, well I needed a change, so I re-enlisted for a

few years. My time just ended, so I'm back here as a civilian again, doing some contract work."

The shifting of his eyes led her to believe there was more to the story, but she didn't press the issue. It felt like prying and that seemed rude after not having seen him for so long.

"Do you sing?" she asked, gesturing at the karaoke book on the table in an attempt to change the conversation.

A small smile pulled at the corner of his lips. "No, but I'd love to hear you sing. I always enjoyed watching you belting it out in the booth."

Unsure how to respond to that tidbit of information, Lanie felt her face flush again. Had Azarius had a crush on her? If so, did he still? And did she want him to? These questions circled through her brain, but all she could manage was, "You watched me?"

"Only a few times," he said. "You always looked like you were having fun, so go ahead and pick something. I'll cheer you on."

Azarius kicked himself as Lanie's auburn head dropped to scan the binder of songs. He had almost spilled how attracted he was to her. He had been for years. In fact, her marriage was what drove him from the station and to re-enlist. Though he'd never gotten up the nerve to tell her how he felt, seeing her married to another had been unbearable.

Now here they were back in the same town and both single. He finally had the chance to show her how he felt, if he didn't mess it up too badly.

"Okay, I think I'll try this one." Lanie pointed to a song in the book.

He smiled and nodded at her as she scribbled the choice on a piece of paper. Azarius didn't care what she sang; she had the voice of an angel any time she opened her mouth.

Lanie stood and made her way to the stage, handing over the piece of paper to the DJ. He scanned it and motioned for her to take the mic on the small raised platform that served as a stage. Looking a little timid, she stood in front of the microphone and offered him a small smile.

Azarius flashed her a thumbs up and smiled as the music started. She probably had no idea the Duran Duran song she chose reminded him of her. He thought back to the day he had accidentally stumbled upon her singing it in the booth.

"Azarius, can you look at the board in control room three?" the station manager asked. "It's been frizzing out again."

"Of course, sir," Azarius said. He grabbed the tool box from the closet that housed it and headed downstairs to the control booths. Lanie was on in control room three, which made the job even more appealing. Azarius didn't believe in love at first sight, but from the moment he had met Lanie, she had affected him in a way no other woman had. Now if he could just get up the courage to tell her.

Duran Duran's "Come Undone" was billowing out of the room as he approached. He knocked on the door, but when the music didn't lower, he assumed she hadn't heard his knock, and he pushed the door open slowly.

Lanie stood behind the board in a pair of cutoff denim shorts and a red tank top. Her auburn hair flowed freely down her shoulders and bounced with the movement of her head from side to side.

Her beautiful soprano voice belted out the lyrics, mesmerizing Azarius. He could have stood there all day watching her. "Can I believe you're taking my... Oh!" Her voice stopped as she turned and spied him standing there. "I'm sorry, I didn't hear you come in."

"That's okay." He smiled and held up the tool box, so she would realize he wasn't being voyeuristic. "I knocked but …" he shrugged. "I need to check out the control panel."

She lowered the music and stepped back. "Of course. You have about two minutes until this song ends though."

"I'll be quick."

"I love singing," she said as if trying to explain her actions. "And since the booth is soundproof, I often test my range since no one can hear me. My singing doesn't go out over the radio."

Azarius bit his lip to hide his smile at her nervousness. "Even if it did, no one would mind," he said. "You have a beautiful voice." He watched the soft pink color climb her face before turning back to the control panel.

"Was it okay?" Lanie asked as she finished the song and returned to the table.

"It was amazing," Azarius said.

A rose color flooded Lanie's cheeks, and she dropped her eyes. "You don't have to say that."

"No, I don't, but you are an amazing singer." Her eyes lifted, and he felt himself falling into the hazel depths. "Lanie, I'd love to hang out with you again," he began. "Are you into eighties music?"

Lanie blinked at him. "Am I into what?"

"Eighties music. I know it sounds silly, but I love to watch old music videos, and I thought maybe you'd like to hang out and watch them with me."

"Like a date?" she asked, one eyebrow arched in the air.

Azarius realized how silly that sounded. Yeah, come hang out and watch videos with me, but it was who he was. "Like two old friends reconnecting," he said. "With the possibility of more."

She smiled at him and placed her hand on his, sending tingles down his arm. "I'd like that. I could use an old friend right about now."

Order your copy today at https://www.books2read.com/loveconquersall

Lorana Hoopes is an inspirational author originally from Texas but now living in the PNW with her husband and three children. When not writing, she can be seen kickboxing at the gym, singing, or acting on stage. One day, she hopes to retire from teaching and write full time.

If you enjoyed this story, be sure to check out Lorana's other books.

When Love Returns : The first in the Star Lake series. Presley Hays and Brandon Scott were best friends in High School until Morgan entered their town and stole Brandon's heart. Devastated, Presley takes a scholarship to Le Cordon Bleu, but five years later, she is back in Star Lake after a tough breakup. Brandon thought he'd never return to Star Lake after Morgan left him and his daughter Joy, but when his father needs help, he returns home and finds more than he bargained for. Can Presley and Brandon forget past hurts or will their stubborn natures keep

them   apart   forever?
http://books2read.com/whenlovereturns

The Power of Prayer: The first in the Heartbeats series. Callie Green thought she had her whole life planned out until her fiance left her at the altar. When her carefully laid plans crumble, she begins to make mistakes at work and engage in uncharacteristic activities. After a mistake nearly costs her her job, she cashes in her honeymoon tickets for some time away. There she meets JD, a charming Christian man who, even though she is not a believer, captures her interest. Before their relationship can deepen, Callie's ex-fiance shows back up in her life and she is forced to choose between Daniel and JD. Who will she choose and how will her choice affect the rest of her life? Find out in this touching novel, the first of the Heartbeats   series.
http://books2read.com/PowerofPrayer

Where It All Began: Sandra Baker thought her life was on the right track until she ended up pregnant. Her boyfriend, not wanting the baby, pushes her to have an abortion. After the procedure, Sandra's life falls apart, and she turns to alcohol. Her relationship ends, and she struggles to find meaning in her life. When she meets Henry Dobbs, a strong Christian man, she begins to wonder if God would accept her. Will she tell Henry her darkest secret? And will she ever be able to forgive herself and find healing? Find out in this emotional love story. http://books2read.com/WhereBegan

When Hearts Collide: Amanda Adams has always been a Christian, but she's a novice at relationships. Her first year in college, she falls for a man she believes cares about her, but he has ulterior motives. Does she miss the signs because of her toxic roommate or for some other reason? Jess Peterson has lived a life of abuse and lost her self worth, but when she meets Amanda, she begins to wonder if there is a loving father looking down on her. Her decisions lead her one way, but when she ends up pregnant, she must make some major changes. Plus, she finds she now has to be the rock for Amanda after her faith is shaken. The third book in the Heartbeats series, this one is a must read for mothers and girls heading to college. Though part of the series, it is a stand alone book and can be read separately. http://books2read.com/Whenheartscollide

A Father's Love: Maxwell Banks was the ultimate player until he found himself caring for a daughter he didn't know he had. Can he change to become the role model she needs? Alyssa Miller hasn't had the best luck with past relationships, so why is she falling for the one man who is sure to break her heart? Though nearly complete opposites, feelings develop, but can Max really change his philandering ways? Or will one mistake seal his fate forever? http://books2read.com/AFathersLove

Love Breaks Through: Brent just wanted to finish his novel in peace, but when his car breaks down in Sweet Grove, he is forced to deal with a female mechanic and try to get along. Sam thought she had given up on city boys, but when Brent shows up in her shop, she finds herself fighting attraction. Will their stubborn natures keep them apart or can a small town festival bring them together?

Her children's early reader chapter book series:

The Wishing Stone #1: Dangerous Dinosaur http://books2read.com/WishingStone1

The Wishing Stone #2: Dragon Dilemma http://books2read.com/WishingStone2

The Wishing Stone #3: Mesmerizing Mermaids http://books2read.com/wishingstone3

www.authorloranahoopes.com
loranahoopes@gmail.com

Printed in Great Britain
by Amazon